What's Cooking in Flowerville?

Recipes from Balconies, Rooftops, and Gardens

TO SOFIA, CHIARA, AND SIMONE,
AND TO ALL THE CHILDREN WHO SPENT
TOO MUCH TIME INSIDE THEIR HOMES.

THANK YOU TO GÉRALDINE AND FRÉDÉRIC,
WITHOUT WHOM THIS BOOK WOULD NOT
HAVE BEEN MADE.

F.S.

What's Cooking in Flowerville?

Recipes from Balconies, Rooftops, and Gardens

Felicita Sala

PRESTEL

MUNICH · LONDON · NEW YORK

SPRING HAS ARRIVED IN FLOWERVILLE.
AT 10 GARDEN STREET, EVERYONE IS BUSY
IN THE GARDEN: DIGGING, PLANTING,
SOWING, AND GATHERING.

APRIL

ASPARAGUS STAND
TALL AND STRONG,
LIKE SOLDIERS
GUARDING THE GARDEN.
BUT HERE COMES MARIA
TO CHOP THEM DOWN!

3 SPRING ONIONS, THINLY SLICED

7 OUNCES (200g) GRUYÈRE OR CHEDDAR, GRATED

10 FRESH ASPARAGUS, ENDS PEELED AND CHOPPED FINELY

3½ OUNCES (100g) PARMESAN, GRATED

3 EGGS

½ TSP SALT

PEPPER, TO TASTE

NUTMEG, TO TASTE

4½ OUNCES (125g) BUTTER, CUT IN SMALL CUBES

2 CUPS (250g) FLOUR (half plain, half wholemeal)

⅓ CUP (80ml) ICE-COLD WATER

1 CUP (250g) HEAVY CREAM OR CRÈME FRAÎCHE

Asparagus Quiche

TO MAKE THE DOUGH, MIX THE FLOUR, BUTTER AND SALT WITH YOUR HANDS. ADD THE WATER AND KNEAD UNTIL SMOOTH. WRAP AND PLACE IN THE FRIDGE FOR HALF AN HOUR. PREHEAT OVEN TO 350°F (180°C). FRY THE ASPARAGUS IN A LITTLE OLIVE OIL UNTIL SOFT, RESERVING THE HEADS FOR DECORATION. WHISK TOGETHER THE EGGS, CREAM, SALT, PEPPER, AND NUTMEG. ADD IN THE SPRING ONIONS, COOKED ASPARAGUS, AND GRUYÈRE OR CHEDDAR. ROLL OUT THE DOUGH UNTIL IT'S SLIGHTLY LARGER THAN THE BAKING DISH. PLACE IT ON THE DISH AND PRESS DOWN THE BOTTOM AND SIDES. POKE THE BOTTOM WITH A FORK. POUR FILLING INTO QUICHE BASE. SPRINKLE WITH THE PARMESAN AND DECORATE WITH ASPARAGUS TOPS. BAKE FOR 45 MINUTES OR UNTIL GOLDEN ON TOP.

SERVES 6

MAY

ON A BALCONY NEARBY,
MRS. THISTLE IS WONDERING
WHAT IT WOULD BE LIKE
TO LIVE INSIDE A GREEN PEA POD,
PERFECTLY ROUND AND COZY AND HAPPY.

3 SHALLOTS, CHOPPED

1 POUND (500g) PEAS, SHELLED

5 GARLIC CLOVES, PEELED and CHOPPED, PLUS 1 FOR THE CROUTONS, PEELED

2 BUNCHES of BASIL LEAVES, ROUGHLY CHOPPED

4 TBSP EXTRA-VIRGIN OLIVE OIL

1 BUNCH of MINT LEAVES, ROUGHLY CHOPPED

1 TSP SALT

PEPPER, TO TASTE

ZEST of 2 LEMONS

3½ OUNCES (100g) FETA

3 CUPS (750ml) VEGETABLE STOCK

Pea, Basil, and Mint Soup

IN A LARGE POT, FRY THE SHALLOTS AND GARLIC UNTIL GOLDEN, STIRRING OFTEN. ADD THE PEAS AND STIR. POUR IN THE STOCK, ADD THE HERBS AND 1 TSP OF SALT, BRING TO THE BOIL, AND COOK FOR 7 MINUTES. BLITZ WITH AN IMMERSION BLENDER UNTIL SMOOTH. MAKE SOME TOAST, RUB A GARLIC CLOVE OVER IT, AND CHOP INTO CROUTONS. PUT THE SOUP IN BOWLS WITH THE CROUTONS, CRUMBLED FETA, LEMON ZEST, PEPPER, A SQUEEZE OF LEMON JUICE, AND A DRIZZLE OF OLIVE OIL.

SERVES 6-8

JUNE

A TREE IS READY TO BE PICKED
ON TAMARIND AVENUE.
SOME CHERRIES ARE USED AS EARRINGS,
SOME AS AMMUNITION,
AND SOME ARE GATHERED
FOR A SPECIAL TREAT.

½ CUP (60g) FLOUR

6 TBSP (75g) SUGAR, PLUS A LITTLE EXTRA FOR PIE DISH

2 CUPS CHERRIES, PITTED

2 EGGS, PLUS 1 YOLK

A PINCH OF SALT

¾ CUP (200ml) MILK

1 TSP VANILLA EXTRACT

2 TBSP (25g) BUTTER

Vanille

Cherry Clafoutis

PREHEAT THE OVEN TO 350°F (180°C). CHOP THE CHERRIES IN HALF AND SPRINKLE WITH 1 TBSP OF SUGAR. GREASE A PIE DISH WITH BUTTER AND SPRINKLE WITH SUGAR. PLACE THE CHERRIES IN THE DISH AND BAKE FOR 5 MINUTES TO SOFTEN THEM. MELT THE BUTTER GENTLY IN A SMALL PAN AND SET ASIDE. IN A BOWL, WHISK THE EGGS, 5 TBSP SUGAR, AND VANILLA. ADD FLOUR AND A PINCH OF SALT AND WHISK UNTIL SMOOTH. ADD MILK AND BUTTER, AND MIX WELL. POUR THE BATTER INTO THE PIE DISH OVER THE CHERRIES AND BAKE FOR 35-40 MINUTES. SERVE WARM WITH A SCOOP OF VANILLA ICE CREAM.

SERVES 6-8

JULY

JUST OUTSIDE THE CITY, CUCUMBERS
HAVE SLOWLY CREPT UP A TRELLIS.
THEY ARE COOL AND CRISP.
TORPEDOS FULL OF WATER ON HOT DAYS.
RAMON IS ABOUT TO FIND OUT
IF THEY CAN FLOAT.

½ TSP
GROUND CUMIN

1½ CUPS
(450g)
FULL FAT
GREEK
YOGURT

1 SMALL
CUCUMBER

YOGURT

2 TBSP
EXTRA-VIRGIN
OLIVE OIL

1 TBSP
LEMON JUICE

1 GARLIC CLOVE,
MASHED TO A PASTE

1 TBSP
FRESH DILL,
MINCED

oil

1 TSP HONEY

½ TSP SALT

Tzatziki

GRATE THE CUCUMBER, SPRINKLE WITH A PINCH OF SALT, AND SQUEEZE THE
WATER OUT THROUGH A SIEVE OR IN A CLEAN CLOTH. COMBINE YOGURT,
GARLIC, OIL, HONEY, CUMIN, LEMON, AND ½ TSP SALT AND LET IT REST IN
THE FRIDGE FOR A COUPLE OF HOURS. ADD CUCUMBER AND DILL AND MIX WELL.
SERVE WITH TOASTED FLAT BREAD.   MAKES 2 CUPS

AUGUST

UP HIGH, CLOSE TO THE SKY, THE SUMMER SUN
MAKES BELL PEPPERS TURN DIFFERENT COLOURS,
LIKE TRAFFIC LIGHTS. INSIDE THEY ARE HOLLOW,
SO THERE IS LOTS OF SPACE TO PUT OTHER THINGS.

2 RED
BELL PEPPERS,
HALVED AND DESEEDED

4 TBSP EXTRA VIRGIN
OLIVE OIL

1 BUNCH
OF PARSLEY,
MINCED

1 TOMATO OR
3 SUNDRIED
TOMATOES, OR
BOTH

3 TSP
CAPERS

8 ANCHOVY FILLETS

1 GARLIC
CLOVE

SALT
AND
PEPPER

2 CUPS
DAY OLD BREAD,
CRUSTS REMOVED,
CUT INTO CHUNKS

Stuffed Peppers

PREHEAT OVEN TO 350°F (180°C). ROUGHLY CHOP THE TOMATOES AND CAPERS, AND MINCE THE GARLIC. IN A BOWL, MIX THE BREAD CHUNKS WITH TOMATOES, CAPERS, GARLIC, ANCHOVIES, PARSLEY, AND OLIVE OIL. ADD ½ TSP OF SALT. LINE AN OVEN TRAY WITH BAKING PAPER, DRIZZLE WITH OLIVE OIL, ADD A PINCH OF SALT AND 2 TBSP OF WATER. FILL THE PEPPER HALVES WITH THE MIX AND PLACE ON TRAY. DRIZZLE GENEROUSLY WITH OLIVE OIL AND BAKE FOR 40-45 MINUTES. SERVE WITH ROAST POTATOES.

SERVES 4

SEPTEMBER

LIKE GREEN AND YELLOW LANTERNS,
PEARS FILL A TREE ON PUMPERNICKEL LANE.
AND NOW THEY'VE FOUND THEIR WAY INSIDE A KITCHEN
TO BE CHOPPED, GRATED, BITTEN, AND SAVORED.
THEY ARE JUICY AND PURE.

2 FIRM PEARS, GRATED

A PINCH OF SALT

3 TBSP SUGAR

1 CUP (250g) RICOTTA

A SPLASH OF LEMON JUICE

2 CUPS (250g) FLOUR

2 EGGS

½ CUP (120ml) MILK

2 TSP BAKING POWDER

Pear and Ricotta Pancakes

MASH THE RICOTTA WITH THE SUGAR. ADD THE EGGS AND BEAT UNTIL SMOOTH. ADD THE GRATED PEARS, MILK, SALT AND LEMON JUICE, AND STIR. ADD THE FLOUR AND BAKING POWDER GRADUALLY AND MIX WELL. LET THE MIXTURE SIT IN THE FRIDGE FOR 1 HOUR. IF THE BATTER IS TOO THICK, ADD A LITTLE MILK AND STIR. POUR 2-3 TBSP OF BATTER ON A HOT PAN WITH SOME BUTTER. TURN EACH PANCAKE AFTER IT STARTS TO FORM BUBBLES AND FINISH COOKING ON THE OTHER SIDE FOR ABOUT 30 SECONDS. SERVE WITH HONEY AND LEMON OR MAPLE SYRUP.

MAKES 12

OCTOBER

IN THIS NEIGHBORHOOD,
MANY SEEDS WERE PLANTED BY MANY HANDS.
IN THEIR PLACE THERE ARE NOW SQUASHES AND PUMPKINS.
THEY SIT ON THE GROUND WITH THEIR HEAVY BOTTOMS,
WAITING TO BE TRANSFORMED INTO CAKES,
SOUPS, OR SCARY FACES.

2.2 POUNDS (1 KILO) BUTTERNUT SQUASH OR PUMPKIN, PEELED AND CUBED

½ CUP (100g) SOFT BROWN SUGAR

2 TBSP FINE BREADCRUMBS

A PINCH of SALT

3 EGGS, BEATEN

2 TBSP (30g) MELTED BUTTER

1 CUP (100g) ALMOND FLOUR

2 CUPS (500ml) WHOLE MILK

1 TSP CINNAMON

ICING SUGAR

A HANDFUL of SLICED ALMONDS

Butternut Squash Cake

SIMMER SQUASH IN MILK OVER LOW HEAT FOR 30 MINUTES OR UNTIL SOFT. DRAIN IN A COLANDER AND LEAVE TO COOL, SQUEEZING OUT EXCESS LIQUID. IN A BOWL, BEAT THE EGGS WITH SUGAR, BUTTER, ALMOND FLOUR, BREADCRUMBS, CINNAMON, AND SALT. STIR IN THE COOKED SQUASH UNTIL SMOOTH. POUR IN A GREASED PIE DISH, SPRINKLE ALMONDS ON TOP AND BAKE IN THE OVEN AT 350°F (180°C) FOR 45-50 MINUTES OR UNTIL GOLDEN. WHEN THE CAKE HAS COOLED DOWN, DUST WITH ICING SUGAR.

SERVES 8-10

NOVEMBER

IN A FANCY GARDEN
IN THE CITY CENTER,
THE EARTH IS HIDING
SOMETHING BRIGHT.
HERE ARE THE BEETS,
UNDER GIANT GREEN UMBRELLAS.
SOPHIE PULLS ONE OUT.
A DEEP PURPLE TROPHY!

3 MEDIUM
BEETS

2 TBSP
TAHINI

1 GARLIC
CLOVE,
MINCED

3 TBSP
FULL FAT
GREEK YOGURT

1 TBSP EXTRA
VIRGIN OLIVE OIL

A
SPLASH OF
LEMON
JUICE

SALT, TO
TASTE

A HANDFUL
OF TOASTED
PINE NUTS

Roasted Beet Dip

PREHEAT OVEN TO 350°F (180°C). PUT BEETS IN A SMALL ROASTING PAN WITH HALF A GLASS OF WATER. COVER WITH FOIL AND BAKE FOR 1 HOUR. LET THE BEETS COOL AND THEN PEEL THEM, CUT THEM INTO CHUNKS, AND PUREE THEM WITH AN IMMERSION BLENDER ALONG WITH THE GARLIC. ADD OLIVE OIL, YOGURT, TAHINI, LEMON JUICE, AND SALT TO TASTE. POUR INTO A BOWL AND SPRINKLE WITH TOASTED PINE NUTS. SERVE WITH TOASTED BREAD.

MAKES 1½ CUPS

DECEMBER

POTATOES ARE STORED
FOR THE WINTER
IN FATIMA'S CELLAR.
THEY LOVE DARK, COOL PLACES.
IT REMINDS THEM OF
WHEN THEY WERE BABIES,
DEEP INSIDE THE EARTH.

2 MEDIUM POTATOES
(APPROX. 9 OUNCES/250g),
PEELED AND CHOPPED

1 CUP (250ml) OF MILK MIXED WITH
2 CUPS (500ml) OF WATER

2 TBSP GRATED PARMESAN

1 EGG

2 BAY LEAVES

10-OUNCE
(300g) COD FILLET
OR OTHER WHITE FISH

1 GARLIC CLOVE,
MINCED

LEMON ZEST

A HANDFUL
OF PARSLEY,
FINELY CHOPPED

3 TBSP BREADCRUMBS

SALT AND
PEPPER

VEGETABLE
OIL

Potato and Cod Croquettes

PUT THE FISH IN A SAUCEPAN AND COVER WITH MILK AND WATER. ADD BAY LEAVES AND BRING TO A BOIL. SIMMER FOR 4 MINUTES AND TAKE OUT THE FISH WITH A SLOTTED SPOON. LEAVE IT TO COOL, THEN CRUMBLE IT WITH A FORK AND TAKE OUT ANY BONES. ADD POTATOES TO THE SAME SAUCEPAN AND COOK UNTIL SOFT. DRAIN THE POTATOES AND PLACE THEM IN A BOWL WITH THE COD. MASH WITH A BIG PINCH OF SALT, THEN MIX IN THE EGG, PARMESAN, PARSLEY, PEPPER, GARLIC, AND A LITTLE LEMON ZEST. MIX WELL UNTIL SMOOTH AND THEN FORM INTO CYLINDERS. COAT THE CROQUETTES IN BREADCRUMBS IN A SHALLOW DISH. HEAT SOME OIL IN A PAN. FRY THE CAKES FOR 3 MINUTES ON EACH SIDE OR UNTIL GOLDEN BROWN. DRAIN, SPRINKLE WITH SALT, AND SERVE WITH A SPLASH OF LEMON AND A DOLLOP OF MAYONNAISE.

MAKES 18

JANUARY

ON A TREE ON A BALCONY ON CAULIFLOWER ROAD,
TINY LEMON SUNS BRIGHTEN A DARK WINTER DAY.
A ROSEMARY BUSH GROWS HERE TOO.
THEY KEEP EACH OTHER COMPANY AND ARE VERY GOOD FRIENDS.

ZEST OF
2 LEMONS

JUICE OF
1 LEMON

1 CUP (200g) DRY CANNELLINI BEANS
(OR 2 CUPS/400g COOKED BEANS, DRAINED)

4 GARLIC
CLOVES

EXTRA-VIRGIN
OLIVE OIL

2 SPRIGS OF FRESH
ROSEMARY

1 CUP BEAN
COOKING LIQUID

olive oi

SALT
AND
PEPPER

Lemony Bean Dip

SOAK THE BEANS IN WATER OVERNIGHT. DRAIN THE BEANS AND COOK IN A POT OF WATER
WITH 1 CLOVE OF GARLIC AND 1 SPRIG OF ROSEMARY FOR 1 HOUR OR UNTIL SOFT. ADD 1 TSP OF
SALT AT THE END AND LET THE BEANS REST, THEN DRAIN THEM, RESERVING 1 CUP OF LIQUID.
FINELY CHOP 3 CLOVES OF GARLIC AND THE LEAVES FROM A SPRIG OF ROSEMARY AND GENTLY
FRY IN OLIVE OIL FOR 2 MINUTES, STIRRING ALL THE WHILE. ADD THE WARM GARLICKY OIL
TO A BOWL WITH THE BEANS AND A FEW TABLESPOONS OF BEAN-COOKING LIQUID.
SQUASH THE MIX WITH A FORK OR PUREE WITH A BLENDER. ADD THE LEMON JUICE,
THE ZEST, SALT, AND PEPPER AND MIX. PLACE IN A BOWL AND DRIZZLE WITH 3 TBSP
EXTRA-VIRGIN OLIVE OIL. SERVE WITH FRESH BREAD.   MAKES 2 CUPS

FEBRUARY

HOW LUCKY TO HAVE AN ORANGE TREE RIGHT BEHIND YOUR HOUSE!
JUICY PLANETS HANG LIKE GIFTS FOR THE CHILDREN OF CINNAMON STREET.
BABY LEO TRIES TO BITE ONE WITH ONLY TWO TEETH, AND FAILS.

3/4 CUP (180 ml) EXTRA-VIRGIN OLIVE OIL

JUICE AND ZEST OF 2 BLOOD ORANGES (ABOUT 1 CUP/200ml OF JUICE)

1 CUP (200g) SUGAR

3 EGGS

1/2 CUP (120 ml) PLAIN YOGURT OR MILK

2 CUPS (250g) FLOUR

1 TSP BAKING POWDER

A PINCH OF SALT

Blood Orange and Olive Oil Cake

PREHEAT THE OVEN TO 350°F (180°C). BUTTER AND FLOUR AN 8- OR 9-INCH (20- OR 23-cm) CAKE TIN. RUB SUGAR AND ORANGE ZEST TOGETHER IN A BOWL. WHISK IN THE EGGS ONE BY ONE. ADD THE YOGURT OR MILK, OLIVE OIL, AND ORANGE JUICE. ADD THE FLOUR, SALT, AND BAKING POWDER AND MIX WELL. POUR INTO CAKE TIN AND BAKE FOR ABOUT 45 MINUTES, OR UNTIL SKEWER COMES OUT CLEAN. LET COOL AND DUST WITH ICING SUGAR.

SERVES 8

MARCH

A FOREST OF HERBS
GROWS INSIDE THIS HOME.
SAMUEL WISHES HE COULD GO
CAMPING IN A REAL FOREST.
"SOON," SAYS GRANDPA.
"WHEN THE RAINY SEASON STOPS."

9 OUNCES (250g) DRY CHICKPEAS

CORIANDER

PARSLEY

DILL

EXTRA-VIRGIN OLIVE OIL

1 GARLIC CLOVE, MINCED

MINT

1 SMALL BUNCH EACH, CHOPPED

1 TBSP FLOUR MIXED WITH 1/2 TSP BAKING POWDER

1/2 RED ONION, FINELY CHOPPED

1 TSP GROUND CUMIN

1/2 TSP GROUND CORIANDER SEEDS

ZEST OF 1 LEMON

1 TSP SALT

VEGETABLE OIL

1/2 CUP TAHINI

JUICE OF 1 LEMON

PEPPER, TO TASTE

1/2 TSP SMOKED PAPRIKA

Herb Falafel with Tahini Sauce

SOAK THE CHICKPEAS OVERNIGHT WITH THE BAKING SODA. DRAIN THE CHICKPEAS AND, IN A MIXER, COMBINE WITH THE GARLIC, ONION, HERBS, AND SPICES. BLITZ UNTIL FINELY GROUND, THEN PLACE IN A BOWL WITH THE SALT AND PEPPER, FLOUR MIXED WITH BAKING POWDER, A DRIZZLE OF OLIVE OIL, AND THE LEMON ZEST. MIX WELL AND SHAPE INTO ROUND BALLS USING ABOUT 2 TSP OF THE MIXTURE FOR EACH ONE, THEN FLATTEN THEM A LITTLE. HEAT THE VEGETABLE OIL IN A DEEP POT AND FRY THE FALAFEL IN BATCHES FOR 1-2 MINUTES ON EACH SIDE UNTIL GOLDEN BROWN. TO MAKE THE SAUCE, WHISK THE LEMON JUICE AND TAHINI TOGETHER WITH A BIG PINCH OF SALT AND PAPRIKA. AS IT COMES TOGETHER, ADD WATER LITTLE BY LITTLE AND WHISK UNTIL SMOOTH AND CREAMY. SERVE FALAFEL WITH THE TAHINI SAUCE AND A GREEN SALAD.

MAKES 18-20

THERE ARE WINTER DAYS WHEN IT SEEMS
THE WHOLE WORLD IS ASLEEP.
SEEDS REST INSIDE THE EARTH,
AND EVEN THE TREES SEEM TO BE WAITING.

THEN ONE DAY, TINY PINK FLOWERS
EMERGE FROM WHO-KNOWS-WHERE.

AND JUST LIKE THE FLOWERS,
PEOPLE COME OUT OF THEIR HOMES AGAIN.
FROM ALL OVER THE CITY THEY COME TOGETHER
FOR THE BIGGEST PICNIC OF THE YEAR.

MUSIC AND BLANKETS
AND BASKETS FULL OF FOOD —
SPRING HAS RETURNED TO
FLOWERVILLE!

GARDENING ACTIONS

SOWING:
THE BIGGER THE SEED, THE DEEPER IT MUST GO: IT SHOULD BE BURIED AT A DEPTH ABOUT TWICE ITS SIZE.

TRANSPLANTING:
ONCE A PLANT HAS GROWN A LITTLE, MOVE IT TO A BIGGER POT OR INTO THE GROUND, SO ITS ROOTS CAN EXPAND.

WATERING:
PLANTS DON'T NEED TOO MUCH WATER. WATER IN THE MORNING OR AT NIGHT, TO KEEP MOISTURE IN.

PEEING IN YOUR WATERING CAN HELPS THE SOIL!

MIXING:
MORE VARIETY IN YOUR GARDEN MEANS PLANTS GET LESS SICK. PLANT VEGETABLES TOGETHER WITH AROMATIC HERBS AND FLOWERS. THIS WILL ATTRACT BEES AND INSECTS, WHO WILL HELP YOUR FRUITS AND VEGETABLES TO GROW!

MULCHING:

BY COVERING THE EARTH WITH STRAW, LEAVES, DRY GRASS, OR WOOD CHIPS, YOU WILL PROTECT THE SOIL, USE LESS WATER, AND STOP WEEDS FROM GROWING.

CARING FOR THE SOIL:

AVOID CHEMICAL FERTILIZERS. MANY THINGS FOUND IN NATURE CAN ENRICH YOUR SOIL, SUCH AS COMPOST, WHICH YOU CAN MAKE FROM FOOD SCRAPS.

RECYCLING:

THERE ARE LOTS OF THINGS YOU CAN RE-USE IN YOUR GARDEN: PAPER AND FOOD SCRAPS FOR COMPOST, JARS AND CANS FOR SEEDLINGS, COOKING WATER FOR WATERING, AND SEEDS FOR PLANTING.

HARVESTING:

PICKING YOUR FRUITS AND VEGGIES IS THE BEST PART OF GARDENING. TIME TO COOK AND SHARE YOUR FOOD!

SHARING:

EXCHANGING PLANTS, SEEDS, AND PRODUCE - AS WELL AS YOUR KNOWLEDGE AND OBSERVATIONS - IS A GREAT WAY TO ENRICH YOUR GARDEN AND HELP SOMEONE ELSE DO THE SAME.

SEEDS

YOU CAN SAVE YOUR OWN FRUIT AND VEGETABLE SEEDS
AND SHARE OR SWAP THEM WITH FRIENDS.

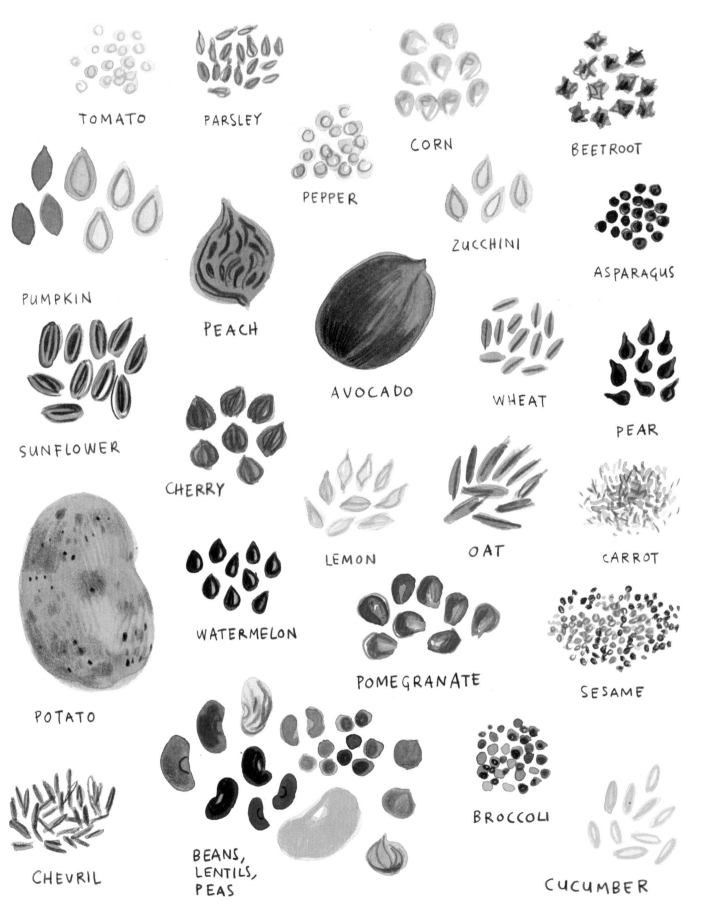

TOMATO

PARSLEY

CORN

BEETROOT

PEPPER

PUMPKIN

ZUCCHINI

ASPARAGUS

PEACH

AVOCADO

WHEAT

SUNFLOWER

PEAR

CHERRY

LEMON

OAT

CARROT

POTATO

WATERMELON

POMEGRANATE

SESAME

CHEVRIL

BEANS,
LENTILS,
PEAS

BROCCOLI

CUCUMBER

GARDENING TOOLS

HERE ARE SOME THINGS YOU CAN USE TO START YOUR OWN VEGETABLE GARDEN. YOU CAN USE TOOLS FROM YOUR HOUSE TOO, LIKE A FORK!

POTS

GOOD SOIL

GARDEN FORK

GARDEN TROWEL

RAKE

SHOVEL

RAISED GARDEN BED

GARDENING GLOVES

RUBBER BOOTS

WATERING CAN

PRUNING SHEARS

FRUITS + VEGETABLES

IT'S GOOD FOR YOU AND GOOD FOR THE EARTH WHEN YOU EAT FRUITS AND VEGGIES THAT ARE IN SEASON. HERE ARE A FEW EXAMPLES:

ASPARAGUS

SWISS CHARD

FAVA BEANS

ARTICHOKE

TURNIP

PEAS

SPINACH

STRAWBERRY

LETTUCE

SPRING ONION

Spring

RADICCHIO

ROSEMARY

THYME

OREGANO

SAGE

DILL

ZUCCHINI

CHERRY

STRING BEANS

Summer

HERBS: ALL YEAR

CUCUMBER

BERRIES

MELONS

PEACH

EGGPLANT

PLUM

BELL PEPPER

TOMATO

KALE

ENDIVE

CABBAGE

KIWI

JERUSALEM ARTICHOKE

CAULIFLOWER

BROCCOLI

DAIKON

PARSLEY

Winter

MINT

BAY LEAF

BASIL

CITRUS FRUIT

LEEK

POTATO

Autumn

MUSHROOMS

FIG

POMEGRANATE

APPLE

GRAPES

SQUASH

CARROT

BEETS

FENNEL

PEAR

CHESTNUT

Library of Congress Control Number: 2021948288
A CIP catalogue record for this book is available from the British Library.

Editorial direction: Constanze Holler
Copyediting: Ayesha Wadhawan
Production management: Susanne Hermann
Handlettering: Felicita Sala
Printing and binding: TBB, a.s.
Paper: Magno Natural

Our production is **climate neutral**
ClimatePartner.com/14044-1912-1001
Print product

Prestel Publishing compensates the CO_2 emissions produced
from the making of this book by supporting a reforestation project in Brazil.
Find further information on the project here:
www.ClimatePartner.com/14044-1912-1001

MIX
Paper from
responsible sources
FSC® C022120

Penguin Random House Verlagsgruppe FSC® N001967
Printed in Slovakia

ISBN 978-3-7913-7518-2
www.prestel.com